BL:
PO ☑ W9-BHR-263
LEXILE:

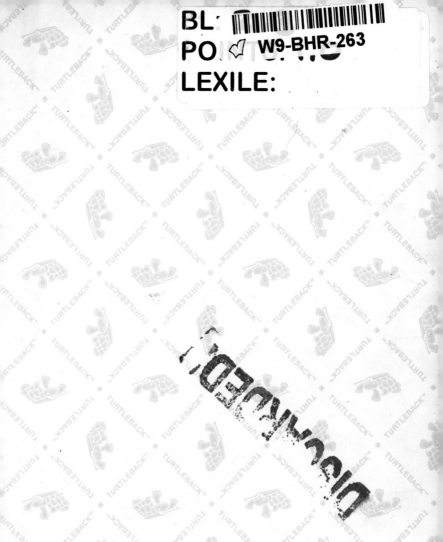

# Ho, Ho, Benjamin, Feliz Navidad

OTHER YEARLING BOOKS
BY PATRICIA REILLY GIFF YOU WILL ENJOY

THE KIDS OF THE POLK STREET SCHOOL

THE BEAST IN MS. ROONEY'S ROOM
FISH FACE
THE CANDY CORN CONTEST
DECEMBER SECRETS
IN THE DINOSAUR'S PAW
BEAST AND THE HALLOWEEN HORROR
EMILY ARROW PROMISES TO DO BETTER THIS YEAR
MONSTER RABBIT RUNS AMUCK!
WAKE UP, EMILY, IT'S MOTHER'S DAY

*Plus the Polk Street Specials:*

WRITE UP A STORM WITH THE POLK STREET SCHOOL
COUNT YOUR MONEY WITH THE POLK STREET SCHOOL
THE POSTCARD PEST
TURKEY TROUBLE

THE LINCOLN LIONS BAND

MEET THE LINCOLN LIONS BAND
YANKEE DOODLE DRUMSTICKS
THE "JINGLE BELLS" JAM
ROOTIN' TOOTIN' BUGLE BOY
THE RED, WHITE, AND BLUE VALENTINE
THE GREAT SHAMROCK DISASTER

YEARLING BOOKS are designed especially to entertain and enlighten young people. Patricia Reilly Giff, consultant to this series, received her bachelor's degree from Marymount College and a master's degree in history from St. John's University. She holds a Professional Diploma in Reading and a Doctorate of Humane Letters from Hofstra University. She was a teacher and reading consultant for many years, and is the author of numerous books for young readers.

For a complete listing of all Yearling titles, write to
Dell Readers Service, P.O. Box 1045,
South Holland, IL 60473.

# Ho, Ho, Benjamin, Feliz Navidad

Friends and Amigos 3

## Patricia Reilly Giff

ILLUSTRATED BY
*DyAnne DiSalvo-Ryan*

c. 1

A Yearling Book

248      LIBRARY
SUTTON ELEMENTARY SCHOOL

45555

Published by
Bantam Doubleday Dell Books for Young Readers
a division of
Bantam Doubleday Dell Publishing Group, Inc.
1540 Broadway
New York, New York 10036

If you purchased this book without a cover you should be aware that this book is stolen property. It was reported as "unsold and destroyed" to the publisher and neither the author nor the publisher has received any payment for this "stripped book."

Text copyright © 1995 by Patricia Reilly Giff
Illustrations copyright © 1995 by DyAnne DiSalvo-Ryan

All rights reserved. No part of this book may be reproduced or transmitted in any form or by any means, electronic or mechanical, including photocopying, recording, or by any information storage and retrieval system, without the written permission of the Publisher, except where permitted by law.

The trademarks Yearling® and Dell® are registered in the U.S. Patent and Trademark Office and in other countries.

ISBN: 0-440-41080-0

Printed in the United States of America

December 1995

10 9 8 7 6 5 4 3 2 1

CWO

*with love to*
*James Martin O'Meara,*
*a new Jim in the family*

## Where to Find the Spanish Lessons in This Book

# DIVIÉRTETE CON EL ESPAÑOL

• • • • • • • • • • • • • • • • • • • • • • • • •

| El tiempo | The Weather |
|---|---|
| *(ehl TYEHM-poh)* | |

| | |
|---|---|
| Hace frío. | It's cold. |
| *(AH-seh FREE-oh)* | |
| | |
| Hace mucho frío. | It's very cold. |
| *(AH-seh MOO-choh* | |
| *FREE-oh)* | |
| | |
| Está nevando. | It's snowing. |
| *(eh-STAH neh-VAHN-doh)* | |
| | |
| Está nevando mucho. | It's snowing a lot. |
| *(eh-STAH neh-VAHN-doh* | |
| *MOO-choh)* | |
| | |
| No está nevando. | It's not snowing. |
| *(NOH eh-STAH* | |
| *neh-VAHN-doh)* | |

# 1

Benjamin Bean looked up at the clock in Room 22.

Five minutes to go until Christmas vacation.

He leaned over to look out the window.

The sky was gray.

He couldn't wait for it to snow.

Next to him, Sarah Cole was writing Spanish words all over her paper.

She was dying to speak Spanish.

She saw him looking.

She slammed her hand over her paper.

"Bet it snows by suppertime," Benjamin said. *"Fantástico."*

Let Sarah know he knew some Spanish, too.

"Bet you're going to end up with a pile of homework," said Mrs. Halfpenny.

Benjamin shot up straight.

He glued his eyes to Mrs. Halfpenny.

That's all he needed. Homework.

He looked at the clock again. Three minutes to go.

Three minutes were forever.

As soon as school was over, he was going home to beg his mother for a dog.

Beg on his hands and knees.

Promise to do the dishes for the next twenty million years.

Promise . . .

"Don't you think so, Benjamin?" Mrs. Halfpenny said.

"I guess so," Benjamin said.

Everyone laughed. Even Mrs. Halfpenny.

Everyone but Sarah.

She clapped her hand on her head. "*Boca grande.* Big mouth."

What was that all about?

Mrs. Halfpenny kept going, though.

She was talking about doing for others.

That was one of her favorite things. That and division.

Benjamin tried to look out the window from the corner of his eye.

All he could see was Sarah's pointy ears.

He dropped his pencil on the floor, and bent down to pick it up.

Good. He could see the whole gray sky. No white drops, though.

"Benjamin," said Mrs. Halfpenny.

He held up his pencil. "Just had to—"

"It's not snowing yet," said Mrs. Half-penny.

"No," said Benjamin.

"It's not going to snow in the next two minutes," said Mrs. Halfpenny.

"I guess not," said Benjamin.

"So instead," said Mrs. Halfpenny, "I'm going to finish telling you . . ."

". . . about doing for others," said Benjamin.

"Yes." Mrs. Halfpenny looked surprised.

Benjamin nodded a little.

On the wall in back of Mrs. Halfpenny was a picture of a puppy.

Benjamin knew exactly what kind of dog he wanted for Christmas.

A big yellow one, just like Sarah's.

Big and strong and powerful.

"When you come back from Christmas,"

said Mrs. Halfpenny, "I want to hear about two things you've done for other people."

No problem, Benjamin thought. He'd already done a pile of stuff.

He had bought his mother a nice comb with a dollar he had found.

He'd bought his father a razor with his birthday money.

All that was left was his little brother, Adam.

Easy. He had two quarters.

The bell rang.

Benjamin raced for his jacket.

He was the first one at the door.

"Don't you want to take any books?" asked Mrs. Halfpenny.

He went back for his math book.

It would be doing for others.

For Mrs. Halfpenny.

Even if he didn't open the book once.

"*Está nevando,*" yelled Sarah.

Benjamin took another look at the sky.

Sarah was right.

It was snowing.

At last.

# DIVIÉRTETE CON EL ESPAÑOL

| **Expresiones** (ex-preh-SYOH-nehs) | **Expressions** |
|---|---|
| ¡Qué bueno! (KEH BWEH-noh) | Oh, goody! |
| ¡Fantástico! (fahn-TAHS-tee-koh) | Fantastic! |
| ¡Caramba! (kah-RAHM-bah) | Wow! |
| ¡Qué sorpresa! (KEH sohr-PREH-sah) | What a surprise! |
| ¡Qué pena! (KEH PEH-nah) | Too bad! |
| ¡Qué pesado! (KEH peh SAH-doh) | How annoying! |
| ¡Cuidado! (kwee-DAH-doh) | Watch out! |
| No importa. (NOH eem-POHR-tah) | Never mind. |

# 2

Benjamin was flying.

His Rollerblades were falling apart, but they were still the fastest blades in Springfield Gardens.

Besides, the snow was dropping down a mile a minute. *La nieve. Está nevando mucho.*

The ground was slippery.

*Fantástico.*

Sarah's dog, Gus, was racing along next to him . . . tongue out, tail wagging.

If he had a dog like Gus, he wouldn't be

afraid of the dark, or the stairs, or the laundry room . . .

The words *la perra* popped into his head. The dog.

His new neighbor, Señora Sanchez, had taught him that when he stopped to pet her dog, Bonita.

She told him Gus was a *perro*.

Señora Sanchez had been a famous artist in Ecuador.

Now she'd probably be famous in Springfield Gardens, too.

Benjamin had followed his mother around for an hour this morning.

Begged for a dog.

Pleaded.

No good.

"There isn't enough room in this apartment for a pet fly," his mother had said.

He could hear someone coming. Sarah.

Benjamin curled up his tongue. He stuck his teeth over his lip.

He whistled. It was loud and screechy. It was a terrific laundry room weapon.

Besides, Sarah couldn't whistle at all.

A sidewalk crack was coming up.

He jumped. Too late.

He landed on his stomach. *Oof.*

Sarah slid to a stop. "Are you all right?"

"*Fantástico,*" he said.

He wasn't all right.

He had scraped his nose and his hands. He probably wouldn't be able to breathe right until he was fifteen.

He'd die before he told Sarah that.

He rolled to his feet.

By this time, Gus was two blocks ahead.

"Come on," Benjamin told Sarah. He took tiny breaths.

He hopped over the curb and sped down Higby Avenue.

Gus was in front of Sarah's mother's bakery.

The bakery window was filled with gingerbread houses.

They looked terrific. They had white icing snow on their roofs, and candy cane fences.

Too bad they tasted like cardboard.

Mannie, the baker, came to the door. "*Buenos días,*" he said.

He handed them a jelly doughnut each.

Benjamin sucked the jelly out of the middle. He looked for a place to throw the rest. "*¡Delicioso!*" Delicious!

Sarah gave him a poke. "Gus eats anything."

Benjamin held out his hand. It felt stiff from where he had scraped it.

Gus took the doughnut in one gulp. He licked the jelly off Benjamin's fingers.

Sarah's mother came to the door. "Mrs. Muñoz, the librarian, is looking for you," she told them.

Benjamin looked at Sarah.

They shook their heads.

Mrs. Cole frowned.

"Well . . . ," Benjamin said.

Sarah nodded.

They started for the library.

Sarah looked back. "Not you, Gus."

Gus watched them for a moment. Then he slid into the bakery before Mrs. Cole closed the door.

Benjamin skated down Library Street.

He knew what Mrs. Muñoz wanted.

She was decorating the library window. Christmas was three days away.

She wanted them to draw pictures.

She wanted them to write wish lists.

In Spanish.

Mrs. Muñoz was in love with Spanish.

She was in love with wasting their whole afternoon.

*¡Qué pesado!*

Benjamin threw himself down on the library steps to unfasten his skates.

Sarah sank down next to him.

Benjamin looked up at the sky. He held his tongue out to catch a few drops.

He wasn't going to get the only thing he wanted for Christmas.

# DIVIÉRTETE CON EL ESPAÑOL

| Feliz Navidad (feh-LEES nah-vee-DAHD) | Merry Christmas |
| --- | --- |
| arbol (AHR-bohl) | tree |
| decoraciones (deh-koh-rah-SYOH-nehs) | decorations |
| luces (LOO-sehs) | lights |
| bastones de Navidad (bah-STOH-nehs deh nah-vee-DAHD) | candy canes |
| Papá Noel (pah-PAH noh-EHL) | Santa Claus |
| deseos (deh-SEH-ohs) | wishes |
| regalos (reh-GAH-lohs) | presents |

3

Mrs. Muñoz smiled the minute she saw them.

Señora Sanchez, Mrs. Muñoz's friend, smiled, too.

She was wearing Christmas tree earrings. They jangled when she moved.

"Laundry room," she told Benjamin, and made a face.

They were the first English words she had learned.

Benjamin had taught them to her when

she had moved into the next-door apartment last week.

"Here's paper," said Mrs. Muñoz. "*Rojo* for Christmas. *Azul* for Hanukkah. *Verde y negro* for Kwanza."

Sarah's little sister, Erica, walked through the door with Thomas Attonichi. "I'll take *amarillo*," she said.

Mrs. Muñoz started to shake her head.

Erica stuck out her lip.

Mrs. Muñoz reached into her desk for the yellow paper. She gave one to Thomas, too. "Just write your Christmas wishes," she said.

"I can't write words yet," said Erica. "Neither can Thomas." They stretched out on the floor. "Don't worry. We'll draw the whole thing."

"All right," said Mrs. Muñoz.

Señora Sanchez came to the table. She

reached for paper and fished in her purse for a colored pencil.

"*Regalos de Navidad,*" she said.

Mrs. Muñoz nodded. "Christmas wishes."

Near Benjamin, Sarah was drawing a bicycle. "I've asked for it every day since last summer."

She tapped her paper. "Bicycle."

Señora Sanchez smiled. She looked at Sarah's paper. "*Sí. Bicicleta.*"

Down on the floor, Erica was working with a purple crayon.

It looked as if she were drawing an elephant. It had huge ears and a trunk.

She saw Benjamin looking.

"Neat, right?" she said. "I'm a very good . . ."

"Artist," Benjamin finished for her.

"It's a pony," she said. "I asked for one last year, too."

Sarah had finished her bicycle. Underneath she was drawing something else.

Benjamin angled his head to get a better look.

"*Español,*" she was writing in curlicue printing.

"I've got to learn Spanish sooner or later," she said. "I want to tell secrets with my friend Anna. I want to write to Luisa in Colombia."

Benjamin nodded. He looked at Thomas's paper.

Thomas was scribbling all over the place.

"What's that?" Benjamin asked.

Thomas was too busy to answer.

Benjamin picked a little stone out of his hand.

He drew a snowman on the corner of his paper.

Too bad he had used a pencil.

A grayish snowman looked kind of silly.

Next to him, Señora Sanchez was looking down at the paper in front of her.

With the green crayon she was drawing trees and grass and a small green house.

She drew a window next.

He leaned closer. It looked as if she was drawing shoes on the windowsill.

Mrs. Muñoz looked at Benjamin. "Yes, they're shoes. *Zapatos.* In Ecuador, children wait for presents in their shoes."

It looked as if Señora Sanchez was crying.

"*¡Qué pena!* My friend misses Ecuador," Mrs. Muñoz said.

Quickly Benjamin looked down at his blank paper.

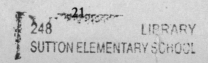
248   LIBRARY
SUTTON ELEMENTARY SCHOOL

He began to draw a huge dog, a dog like Gus.

A dog that would come with him everywhere . . . in the dark, down the stairs, into the laundry room.

He took another quick look at Señora Sanchez.

She looked up, too.

Benjamin could see the tears in her eyes.

She smiled at him anyway. She pointed to his paper. *"Perro."*

Benjamin nodded.

He felt a little like crying, too.

# DIVIÉRTETE CON EL ESPAÑOL

• • • • • • • • • • • • • • • • • • • • • • •

## Los deseos de Erica y de Tomás
*(lohs deh-SEH-ohs deh
EH-ree-kah ee deh toh-MAHS)*

| Los deseos de Erica | Erica's Wishes |
| --- | --- |
| caballito *(kah-bah-YEE-toh)* | pony |
| creyones *(kreh-YOH-nehs)* | crayons |
| muñeca *(moo-NYEH-kah)* | doll |
| rompecabezas *(rohm-peh-kah-BEH-sahs)* | puzzle |
| sorpresas *(sohr-PREH-sahs)* | surprises |

| Los deseos de Tomás | Thomas's Wishes |
| --- | --- |
| patines *(pah-TEE-nehs)* | skates |
| pelota *(peh-LOH-tah)* | ball |
| camiones *(kah-MYOH-nehs)* | trucks |
| tambor *(tahm-BOHR)* | drum |

# 4

It was almost dark by the time Benjamin reached the apartment.

Fat white flakes of snow swirled around the streetlight.

He looked up the street.

No one was around. Good.

The snow was coming down hard.

*Nieve.* He hoped it would snow a hundred inches. . . . *¡Mucha nieve!*

In front of him was the fire escape ladder. He jumped for it.

Not high enough.

He tried again.

His hand slid off the iron rung.

On the third try he felt the rung under his hands.

He hung there for a moment, swinging a little. "Hee ha!" he yelled.

Then he started to climb.

Up one flight, he stopped at Señora Sanchez's window.

She was sitting on the couch.

She still looked sad.

He rubbed the window to see better.

She looked up, and jumped.

"It's just me," he said.

She looked as if she was scared to death.

Then he remembered.

The only words she knew in English were *laundry room*.

He banged on the window. *"Hola,"* he yelled. "It's me."

What was "it's me" in Spanish? he wondered.

Then she saw who it was.

She smiled. *"Benjamín. ¡Qué sorpresa!"* His name sounded strange, like Behn-hah-MEEN. He liked the sound of it.

He nodded.

He climbed up another step.

Underneath, she opened the window. *"Cuidado,"* she said.

He knew what she must be saying.

"Don't worry," he said as loud as he could. "I'll watch out."

No good.

No matter how loud he was, she couldn't understand.

He waved at her.

Then he kept going, up one floor, to his apartment.

He took a quick look through his kitchen window.

Petey the Parrot was squawking on top of his cage. He never went inside except to eat.

The hamster was rushing around on his wheel.

The three goldfish were half asleep in their tank on the counter.

The kitchen was as big as a closet.

Benjamin took another step to his bedroom window and shoved it up.

The bedroom was small, too. There was just enough room for two beds. His and his little brother Adam's.

There wasn't even enough room to walk.

He ducked his head and jumped in.

He landed on his bed.

"Benjamin?" his mother called.

He stopped to reach under his pillow.

He had left a gooey pink candy there.

It was from Señora Sanchez. *Dulce,* she called it.

Gone.

Maybe he'd stuck it under his bed.

His feet were muddy. Good thing the quilt was brown.

He hopped onto Adam's bed and jumped into the hall.

"Didn't I tell you that was dangerous?" his mother called.

"Hey," said Benjamin.

In the living room a tree took up most of the space.

The whole place smelled like Christmas.

His mother was stringing a mess of popcorn.

Adam was eating it from the end of the string as fast as he could.

"Great tree," said Benjamin.

"It's for Crimnis," said Adam. He had pink stuff stuck to his chin.

*Dulce.*

"Did you . . . ," Benjamin began.

"Dangerous," his mother said. "Climbing up that ladder."

"How about a dog?" he asked. "I wouldn't climb the fire escape if I had a dog like Gus."

His mother grinned. "You'd have to live on the fire escape if you had a dog like Gus."

It was no good.

He thought of Mrs. Halfpenny. He'd have to ask his father. Beg . . .

"You buy me a present for Crimnis?" Adam asked.

Benjamin nodded. He'd be able to do a lot of stuff for his mother if he had a dog.

Go to the store in the dark.

Put the clothes in the laundry room dryer.

He thought of Mrs. Halfpenny. He'd have a ton of doing for others.

"Look." Adam grabbed Benjamin's hand.

Across the street, the firehouse door was open.

Benjamin could see the fire truck.

Adam pointed. "That."

A fire truck.

More money than he had thought.

Adam was still pointing. "For Crimnis."

Benjamin nodded. "I guess so."

"With the light."

More money.

Mrs. Halfpenny would love it.

Doing for others.

# DIVIÉRTETE CON EL ESPAÑOL
• • • • • • • • • • • • • • • • • • • • • • •

## Los deseos de Sara y de Adán
### (lohs deh-SEH-ohs deh SAH-rah ee deh ah-DAHN)

| Los deseos de Sara | Sarah's Wishes |
| --- | --- |
| bicicleta (*bee-see-KLEH-tah*) | bicycle |
| pulsera (*pool-SEH-rah*) | bracelet |
| libros (*LEE-brohs*) | books · |
| juegos (*HOOEH-gohs*) | games |
| Quiero hablar español. (*KYEH-roh ah-BLAHR eh-spah-NYOHL*) | I want to speak Spanish. |

| El deseo de Adán | Adam's Wish |
| --- | --- |
| bomba (*BOHM-bah*) | fire truck |

# 5

Benjamin was swimming . . . swimming without water, he told himself.

First he reached out with one arm, then with the other.

He inched his way along under his bed.

He could hear his mother calling from the kitchen. "Benjamin . . ."

He could feel dust, and a Power Ranger, and then, at last, two dimes, and a nickel.

"Benjamin?"

Not enough for Adam's present.

Maybe in his closet.

"If I have to call one more . . ."

Benjamin wiggled out from under the bed.

He slid into the hall.

"I'm right here," he said.

His mother was standing in the bathroom.

She was stuffing bath towels and washcloths into a bag.

"I have to go to Hennie's for Adam's present," he said. "I'm going right this min—"

His mother looked up. "I need you to throw these in a washing machine downstairs."

"How about later?" he said. "How about this afternoon?"

How about never? he wanted to say.

"How about now?" His mother reached

into her pocket. She handed him a pile of quarters.

Benjamin sighed.

His mother was tougher than Mrs. Half-penny.

He stamped back into his bedroom.

He looked through his old school pants.

A dime.

He ran his hands along the shelf.

Two pennies.

On the closet floor, a dollar, crumpled up.

"Hee haa," he said. He reached for his jacket.

He said good-bye to his mother in the kitchen, clucked at the parrot, and waved at Adam, who was in the closet with the pots.

Then he dragged the bag of towels out the door and down the back stairs.

He went slowly, looking over his shoulder.

Only one light was on today.

There were lots of noises in the stairway.

Creaks. Steps. Other things.

"Nothing there," he said. "Nobody there."

"Safe as in your own bed." That was what his mother always said.

His own bed wasn't all that safe.

A thing could come right up the fire escape, sneak open the window, and . . .

"Springfield Gardens is the safest place in the world," his father always said.

The basement wasn't dark.

It was light . . . and shiny.

Eddie, the super, had just painted the whole thing yellow.

It was still scary.

Benjamin tiptoed down the hall, listening.

He pictured Gus, a dog like Gus, marching down the hall with him.

Growling.

Nobody would fool around with a kid who had a dog like that.

A whirring noise came from the laundry room.

Just a dryer.

He stopped at the laundry room door.

He peered around the corner.

Nobody there.

He raced inside and fished around in the bag for the box of soap.

He had forgotten it.

He'd have to go back upstairs for it.

He heard noises in the hall.

Too bad about the soap.

He pulled the towels out of the bag as fast as he could.

There were strange clicking sounds, and something dragging.

He shoved the towels into the nearest washing machine.

The clicking sound was louder now, and there was that other sound. A strange, terrible . . .

He raced down the aisle to the back of the laundry room and dived behind the last dryer.

Someone was at the door.

Someone not moving, not making a sound.

Then the clicking sound came closer.

He opened his mouth.

His mother would never hear him scream.

He screamed anyway.

Someone else was screaming, too.

He took a peek. Bonita, Señora Sanchez's fat little dog, was standing in front of him.

And Señora Sanchez was leaning against the door.

*"Ay ay ay,"* she was yelling at the top of her lungs.

# DIVIÉRTETE CON EL ESPAÑOL

| **Descripciones** *(deh-skree-PSYOH-nehs)* | **Descriptions** |
|---|---|
| Gus es grande. *(gus EHS GRAHN-deh)* | Gus is big. |
| Bonita es pequeña. *(boh-NEE-tah EHS peh-KEH-nyah)* | Bonita is small. |
| Gus es fuerte. *(gus EHS FWEHR-teh)* | Gus is strong. |
| Bonita es débil. *(boh-NEE-tah EHS DEH-beel)* | Bonita is weak. |
| Gus es delgado. *(gus EHS dehl-GAH-doh)* | Gus is thin. |
| Bonita es gorda. *(boh-NEE-tah EHS GOHR-dah)* | Bonita is fat. |
| Gus es guapo. *(gus EHS GWAH-poh)* | Gus is handsome. |
| Bonita es bonita. *(boh-NEE-tah EHS boh-NEE-tah)* | Bonita is pretty. |

# 6

It was lunchtime, and snowing hard.

Benjamin wasn't hungry, though.

He had spent an hour in Señora Sanchez's apartment. Drawings covered the walls. There was one of Erica and Thomas on the library floor. There was one of Bonita eating a bowl of popcorn. There was even one of Benjamin.

Señora Sanchez had opened a box of cookies and stirred hot chocolate on the stove for them.

All the time she spoke in Spanish.

She pointed to one of the pictures.

It showed trees and green plants.

The sun was shining.

Señora Sanchez pointed out the window and shivered.

Benjamin knew what she was saying . . . even though he didn't understand one word.

She was lonesome for her old home.

Benjamin had talked a mile a minute, too.

He told her about being afraid of the laundry room, and the dark, and how he needed a dog.

He took the last pink *dulce* from a plate on the table.

It was great to talk with someone who didn't understand you, he thought. You could say anything you wanted.

Bonita had clicked her toes across the

kitchen floor for a while. Then she had stopped to eat about six cookies.

She had slurped up her own bowl of cocoa.

Bonita was the smallest dog Benjamin had ever seen, and the roundest.

"*Perritos,*" Señora Sanchez had said.

"Dog," said Benjamin.

Right now he banged open the lobby door.

Outside, everything was white.

Almost white.

A little grass was poking up through the snow.

He looked at the sky.

Maybe it would snow again later.

He slid down the path, and headed for the stores.

Lights were twinkling in every window along Higby Avenue.

He could hear the Rudolph song. It was coming from the Make Music store, and someone was ringing bells on the corner.

Gus was sitting at the front door wagging his tail.

He followed Benjamin inside.

Sarah was helping Mannie, the baker. They were putting little candies on a tray. They looked like Señora's Sanchez's *dulces*.

"Want one?" Mannie asked.

"No, thanks." He didn't think he'd eat anything more for a week.

He bent over to give Gus a pat. "Want to go shopping?"

"For *Navidad*?" Sarah reached into her pocket. "I have a list. I wrote it in Spanish . . . for practice."

Mannie looked over her shoulder. "A goat for Erica?" he asked.

Sarah looked down at her list. "A goat? Of course not." She bit at her lip.

Mannie pointed with one fat finger.

"It's supposed to be a pony. A stuffed pony for Erica."

Mannie shook his head and laughed. *"Un caballito,"* he said.

Benjamin could see that Sarah's face was red. "Come on," he said. "Let's go shopping. *Vamos.*"

Sarah reached for her jacket.

Benjamin gave Gus one last pat; then they crossed the street and went into Hennie's.

"Shoppers' Sale" was booming out of a loudspeaker. "Two chocolate Santas for the price of one."

"Great," said Sarah. "I'll get that for Erica, instead of the pony. "One for Erica . . . and I'll eat the other one."

She waited while the salesclerk put them in a bag.

"Wait a minute," Sarah said. "I can't eat that. I have to give it away. I'm trying to do for others. I have only one thing for Mrs. Halfpenny, so far."

"I have two . . . presents for my mother and father," Benjamin said. "I'm going to get a fire truck for . . ."

Sarah looked at him. She was shaking her head. "Not Christmas presents. They don't count, remember?"

Benjamin frowned. "No."

He felt the money in his pocket. "Listen," he said. "I'm spending my last cent on a fire truck for Adam. You don't think that's a do-good?"

The whole time she was making a face. "You were the one who said . . . I knew you weren't paying attention to Mrs. Half-

48

penny. She even asked if Christmas presents should count."

He tried to think back. All he could remember was waiting for snow. *Nieve.*

And Mrs. Halfpenny asking him something.

"Did I say that?" he asked.

*"Boca grande,"* Sarah said.

"Big mouth," he said. "You're right." He thought about doing two good things.

It would take up his whole vacation.

# DIVIÉRTETE CON EL ESPAÑOL
• • • • • • • • • • • • • • • • • • • • • • •

| **Los deseos de Benjamín** (lohs deh-SEH-ohs *deh behn-hah-MEEN*) | **Benjamin's Wishes** |
| --- | --- |
| Quiero un perro. *(KYEH-roh oon PEH-rroh)* | I want a dog. |
| No quiero un pez. *(noh KYEH-roh oon PEHS)* | I don't want a fish. |
| Necesito un perro. *(neh-seh-SEE-toh oon PEH-rroh)* | I need a dog. |
| ¡No necesito un pez! *(NOH neh-seh-SEE-toh oon PEHS)* | I don't need a fish! |

# 7

It was Christmas Eve morning.

The parrot was sitting on top of Benjamin's head, pulling his hair.

"A dog could sleep in my bed," he told his father.

He had asked Sarah about that, about where Gus liked to sleep.

"On top of my feet," Sarah had said.

It sounded wonderful. A dog at his feet every night.

"Yaya yaya," Adam was screeching. He was louder than the parrot.

"Can you hear me?" Benjamin asked his father. "I said, 'a dog . . .' "

Benjamin's father was lying on the floor under the tree. He was singing, "I'll be home for Christmas."

He was working on their train set . . . trying to make it curve around the tree.

He stopped singing. "How about another fish?"

Something was bothering Benjamin, something besides the dog.

He couldn't even think about what it was.

Something sad . . . something about the song?

Adam went over and sat on their father's back. "Benjie got me a fire truck for Crimnis," he said.

"Maybe not," said Benjamin.

Adam looked as if he was going to cry.

"It's supposed to be a surprise," Benjamin said.

"It's out there." Adam pointed toward the window.

Benjamin smiled to himself. He had sneaked the fire truck up the fire escape yesterday.

It was under the bed, way back with the dustballs and last summer's sneakers.

He thought about the sneakers.

How could he be sad about sneakers?

He leaned his head against the window.

Across the street, the fire engine was pulling out.

One of the men saw him and waved.

Benjamin waved back.

Then he saw Señora Sanchez walking up the street.

She had a kerchief over her head, and a million scarves. Still, she looked cold.

She was carrying a bag of groceries.

He banged on the window.

She looked up and smiled. *"Un perrito,"* she called, before she disappeared into the lobby.

Benjamin watched his father for a minute.

"A dog could . . . ," he began and stopped.

He knew what was making him sad.

It was Señora Sanchez.

How terrible to be in a new place for Christmas.

The picture she had drawn at the library popped into his mind.

The house with the shoes on the windowsill.

The house with the sun beating down, and the woman working in the garden.

Adam brought his father to the window now.

Adam was pointing. "Mine for Crimnis. From Benjamin."

Their father was smiling a little, shaking his head. "Not that one."

Benjamin stood up.

For a minute, he didn't know what they were talking about.

"You mean that one?" he asked Adam. "That real one? I didn't . . ."

Before he could finish, Adam's lip was coming out.

"*¡Caramba!*" Benjamin said.

Adam was screaming now.

Adam had wanted a real fire engine, the one that was pulling out right now, lights flashing, sirens screaming.

# DIVIÉRTETE CON EL ESPAÑOL

| La comida de Navidad (lah koh-MEE-dah deh nah-vee-DAHD) | Christmas Dinner |
| --- | --- |
| pavo (PAH-voh) | turkey |
| jamón (hah-MOHN) | ham |
| papas (PAH-pahs) | potatoes |
| salsa (SAHL-sah) | gravy |
| pan (PAHN) | bread |
| pastel (pah-STEHL) | pie |
| postre (POH-streh) | dessert |
| ¡Qué rico! (KEH REE-coh) | Yummy! |

It was after lunch.

Benjamin's mother was running around the kitchen like crazy.

Cranberry sauce was boiling on the stove.

A pile of chestnuts was in a bowl on the sink.

Chestnuts for the stuffing.

His mother swooped down and gave him a hug. "Out of here," she said. "I've got to get a turkey ready."

Outside, the sun was shining.

It was sparkling on the snow.

Icicles dripped from the tops of the windows.

Benjamin had a dollar in his pocket.

His mother had given it to him for cleaning the parrot cage.

The worst job in the world.

He had scraped the bottom of the cage with an old knife in one hand.

He had held his fingers over his nose with the other.

Never mind. *No importa.*

It was his first do-good.

He stopped to kick at a pile of snow.

He had asked his mother if a do-good counted when you were paid for it.

She had thought for a minute. "I was going to give you a dollar anyway," she had said.

Benjamin stood in front of the apartment for a few minutes.

It was freezing cold. *Frío.*

He tucked his chin into his collar.

He walked up Higby Avenue.

Gus was sitting in front of the bakery.

Benjamin threw a snowball in the air.

Gus jumped for it.

"Great dog," Benjamin said.

It was true. Gus was the greatest dog in the world.

And something else was true.

Benjamin wasn't going to get a dog for Christmas.

He'd probably get another fish for the tank.

Maybe he'd get a baseball.

And new Rollerblades.

But there really wasn't room for the dog.

He reached over to pet Gus.

No, he wasn't going to get a dog.

And Adam wasn't going to get a real fire truck.

And Señora Sanchez wasn't going to have Christmas at all. *¡Qué pena!*

Sarah knocked on the bakery window. "Come on in," she called to Benjamin.

Benjamin opened the door. He listened to the bells tinkling.

Benjamin went into the back with Sarah.

The bakery smelled wonderful.

Mannie was taking rolls out of the oven. *"Feliz Navidad,"* he told Benjamin.

Sarah's mother was at the table. She was icing a coffee cake.

Even Erica and Thomas Attonichi were there.

They were making little men out of left-over dough.

"I know this guy doesn't look so hot," Erica told Benjamin. "It's the best I can do."

She reached for a raisin and stuck it into the middle of the doughman's stomach.

Her mother laughed. "I'm not so crazy about this coffee cake, either."

Benjamin sat on one of the stools.

Sarah slid a plate of nuts across to him.

"All your Christmas shopping finished?" Sarah's mother asked.

Sarah reached across for one of the nuts. "How about your do-goods?"

Benjamin shook his head.

He watched Erica finish up her dough-man.

And then he thought of something.

He slid off the stool.

"No," he said. "I still have some shopping to do."

He pulled out a dollar.

"I need a *dulce* first," he said. "Then I have to go to the firehouse."

# DIVIÉRTETE CON EL ESPAÑOL

| Emociones (eh-moh-SYOH-nehs) | Feelings |
|---|---|
| contento (kohn-TEHN-toh) | happy |
| triste (TREE-steh) | sad |
| enojado (eh-noh-HAH-doh) | angry |
| sorprendido (sohr-prehn-DEE-doh) | surprised |
| Estoy contento. (eh-STOY kohn-TEHN-toh) | I am happy. |
| Benjamín está triste. (behn-hah-MEEN eh-STAH TREE-steh) | Benjamin is sad. |
| Sarah está sorprendida. (SAH-rah eh-STAH sohr-prehn-DEE-dah) | Sarah is surprised. |

## 9

It was Christmas . . . the busiest day of Benjamin's life.

Everyone had been up early, even before it was light.

Benjamin had gotten a million presents.

A blue fighting fish in its own small tank.

New Rollerblades.

A computer game.

A bunch of other stuff.

No dog, of course.

His mother and father had loved their presents.

At the end, Benjamin had given Adam the fire truck.

"This one is for you," he had said.

But before Adam had time to say a word, Benjamin had taken him to the window.

"You're going on the fire truck today," he had said. "After dinner."

Adam's eyes opened very wide. "For Crimnis."

Benjamin nodded. "It was the best I could do."

"Good," Adam said. He had given Benjamin a Christmas present, too.

A half-eaten *dulce*.

Benjamin's *dulce* from the other day.

Benjamin smiled.

It was probably the best Adam could do, too.

Right now his mother was setting the table.

She was setting an extra plate.

Yesterday he had asked her to invite Señora Sanchez.

"That's the greatest idea you've ever had," she had told him.

He was on his way downstairs to Señora Sanchez's for the second time.

He opened the door and raced down the stairs.

This morning he had used the fire escape.

He had sneaked down with the sneaker he had found under his bed.

It was filled with *dulces*, and colored pencils, and a dog bone for Bonita.

Right now Señora Sanchez's door was open.

She was waiting for him, smiling.

The sneaker was in her hand.

She was crying again.

"*Muchísimas gracias, Benjamín,*" she said. "*Muy bien. ¡Qué bueno!*"

Benjamin ducked his head.

Suddenly he realized it was a do-good.

He hadn't even thought of it.

Señora Sanchez took his hand.

She led him into the kitchen. "*Perritos,*" she said.

Benjamin shook his head. "Dog," he said when he saw Bonita in the basket.

He looked again.

Two tiny puppies were in the basket with Bonita.

The smallest dogs in the world. *Pequeños.*

"One for you," said Señora Sanchez. "One for me."

"My mother . . . ," Benjamin began.

"*Tu madre . . . sí,*" said Señora, nodding.

He heard his mother and father in the room. Adam came, too.

"It's a very small dog," said his mother.

"And a big surprise," said his father.

For a quick moment, Benjamin thought about a big dog like Gus.

Then one of the puppies raised his head.

It was the greatest dog he had ever seen.

"Tiny," he said. "I think I'll call him . . . Perro."

Outside, Benjamin could hear the fire truck.

It was the greatest Christmas he had ever had.

He reached down to pet the puppy.

"*Feliz Navidad*, Perro," he said.

Señora Sanchez smiled. "Merry Christmas," she said.

| DATE DUE | | |
|---|---|---|
|  |  |  |
|  |  |  |
|  |  |  |
|  |  |  |
|  |  |  |
|  |  |  |
|  |  |  |
|  |  |  |
|  |  |  |
|  |  |  |
|  |  |  |
|  |  |  |
|  |  |  |
|  |  |  |

DISCARDED

45555

GIF

Giff, Patricia
Reilly.

Ho, ho, Benjamin,
feliz navidad

c/

SUTTON ELEMENTARY LIBRARY
HOUSTON TX 77074

556377 00896 51525B 01742E